Yael! I didn't know what th. W9-BKC-791
I got it for you but I just skimmed
through and I'm scared you're a
catalyst for someone that will one
day participate in a women's
march 😐 Anyways... COEXIST!

To women... I guess?

With love and confusion,
DH (that stands for
Daniella Hematian. when
I get married it'll
probably change —
because I will conform
and take my husbands
last name)

Love you
Yael Victoria! ♡
You can seriously change the world!
Update: I just read a little of
this and its very empowering
OMG

milk and honey

milk and honey

rupi kaur

**Andrews McMeel
Publishing**®

a division of Andrews McMeel Universal

Andrews McMeel Publishing
a division of Andrews McMeel Universal
1130 Walnut Street, Kansas City, Missouri 64106

www.andrewsmcmeel.com
www.rupikaur.com

16 17 18 19 20 SDB 10 9 8 7 6 5 4 3 2

ISBN: 978-1-4494-8313-5

Library of Congress Control Number: 2015946719

ATTENTION: SCHOOLS AND BUSINESSES
Andrews McMeel books are available at quantity discounts
with bulk purchase for educational, business, or sales promotional use.
For information, please e-mail the Andrews McMeel Publishing
Special Sales Department: specialsales@amuniversal.com.

for
the arms
that hold me

the
foreword

i don't feel like the girl who wrote *milk and honey*
anymore.
i feel like her mother. or her grandmother
close enough to her. but not her
the girl who wrote this was so young. naive.
eyes like the mouths of fish wide open with wanting
the entire process of writing the pages that follow was
otherworldly. she was otherworldly.
like a beautiful extraterrestrial who does not belong on
this planet
but found herself on it
she had the capacity to consume the entire world with
her fist.
the girl who wrote *milk and honey* saved my life.
she was born. left. and lives within these pages.

———

today is may 10 2016. 6:33 p.m.
i feel older than i did when this journey started. more
tired. exhausted. weathered.
but a lot more sure of myself. with a better sense of what
i'm doing and why.
i am a body within a body. more than one life at once.
every day a new person becomes inside me
i think this is what growth feels like
what do you say when the book with your name on it is
so beyond your name
how do you reflect on a creation that was so natural it
spilled out of you like blood.

when the poems came like bullets
i pulled the words out of me
like the remains of a gunshot.
i had no choice. otherwise i'd rot.
the poems absorbed me. and i absorbed the poems.
the way a fetus soaks in an amniotic sac
how the ocean swallows its swimmer
i was hungry.

milk and honey is what my pain sounds like.
how i cry. also my joy.
i have watched it become our collective journey
how we mourn. smile. grieve. rejoice.

now i'm going to tell you how i came to write this book.

———

in 1992 i am born in a village called munak kalan in the
state of punjab. right below kashmir in northern india. the
month of october. *barsaat*—monsoon season.

accompanying my mother to the hospital is a long row
of relatives. grandparents aunts sisters uncles brothers.
missing from this bouquet of flowering faces is my father.
he is at a friend's apartment in delhi preparing to flee for
canada as a refugee. upon hearing the news of my arrival
he sends johnson's baby products back to the village. to
this day my mother reminds me of that splurge if i ever
question his love for me.

for my father opportunity and time align a month after
i am born. he takes his chance. knowing if he does not
leave now he will end up imprisoned like his friends.
tortured. dead. or perhaps all three in that same sequence.
for the sake of survival my family becomes a footnote in
history. one of those tens of thousands of punjabi sikhs
fleeing punjab because of genocide.

three and a half years later my mother and i join him.
leaving behind three and a half years of the warmest sun
my body has ever known. you get on a plane and all of it
is gone. your clattering language. scorching summers that
are unbearable now but will be nostalgic in the decades
to come. the way village farm green meets city industry
brown. melanin dancing madly on skin. grandparents
you've made into parents.

the displacement is jarring. you are in grandpa's arms at
airport security one minute. both of you weeping like two
rivers joining to make one. suddenly mumma tears you
apart from him for the last time. it's a life ending. and you
have no idea what's about to come.

hours later the wheels of the plane meet the tarmac in
wintery montreal. mumma and i walk out the gate to
baggage claim. men i do not recognize greet us. i cry
when one of them picks me up. mumma tells me he is
my father.

what a word that is. oh the weight it carries.

the adjustment is like putting on clothes a few sizes too big for me. this new world doesn't fit right.

the emotional climate in our montreal apartment is cold. we have less of everything here. less money. space. love. room for error. so much hard physical labor from my parents and nothing to show for it. english doesn't warm up to my tongue until late elementary. one day i try to tell my teacher i need to visit the bathroom but she sends me back to my seat where i end up unable to hold it. it is horrific. when mumma comes to pick me up she asks why i smell.

toys are an unseen luxury. but books. my parents put any extra money we have toward books. either from the local thrift store or the school catalog that forever has a $2.99 item on the front page mumma would never deny me.

as the years pass i learn more english. and remember less punjabi. i am an overstretched bridge between two countries. my limbs scattering in two places at once.

when i begin writing poetry in high school i have a deep desire to write in my mother tongue. there is a beauty in its design. *gurmukhi* a script in which punjabi is written only uses the period. there is no other punctuation. all letters are treated the same. no distinction between upper and lowercase. i enjoy this simplicity. how symmetrical and absolutely straightforward. for a while i try to write poetry in punjabi. but i fail because i cannot utilize the language viscerally enough. i wonder to myself what might happen if i include some of its characteristics in my english work. just periods. all lowercase. this is how the design of *milk and honey* is born.

i write a poem about the 1984 genocide of sikhs in india. there is a line about the women who lived through it. their resilience is breathtaking. they are the enduring survivors to the murders of their husbands and children. the survivors of betrayal. rape. torture. i write that they come out of that terror as smooth as milk and as thick as honey. this is how the title of *milk and honey* is born.

i explore poetry deeper than i ever have. what was it that made these women into milk and honey. that smooth. that thick. why is mumma as resilient as she is. in exploring my own womanhood i think about the pains that have affected those around me.

my thoughts go to the sexual violence we endure as south asian women. we know it intimately. from thousands of years of shame and oppression. from the community and from colonizer after colonizer. by the time i am born i have already survived the first battle of my life. against female feticide. i am one of the lucky ones who has been allowed to live. we are taught our bodies are not our property. you will do with them as your parents wish until they pass the property onto your husband and his family. a good indian girl is quiet. does as she is told. sex does not belong to her. it is something that happens to her on

her wedding night. our job is to lay obediently. not to
enjoy. let him take.

our trauma escapes the confines of our own times.
we're not just healing from what's been inflicted onto
us as children. my experiences have happened to my
mother and her mother and her mother before that. it is
generations of pain embedded into our souls.

i read hundreds of books growing up. but none can
explain this torment to me. i need access to words written
by people who look like me writing about the things i am
going through. at that moment i realize the importance
of representation and know this must be different for my
children. they must have access to their own literature.

———

the girl who wrote *milk and honey* became the writer
that three-and-a-half-year-old girl stumbling down that
montreal tarmac needed.

what gave her the right to write. who told her she could
write about the things that had defined her.

sex. love. violence. fear. race. loss. migration. language.
healing.

she wrote of experience. her own. her family's. her
people's. she did it fearlessly. honestly.

i hope your eyes fall in love with the poems. i hope the milk spills through you and the honey sweetens the way. thank you for holding my heart in your hands.

love and light

—rupi kaur

contents

my heart woke me crying last night
how can i help i begged
my heart said
write the book

the
hurting

how is it so easy for you
to be kind to people he asked

milk and honey dripped
from my lips as i answered

cause people have not
been kind to me

the first boy that kissed me
held my shoulders down
like the handlebars of
the first bicycle
he ever rode
i was five

he had the smell of
starvation on his lips
which he picked up from
his father feasting on his mother at 4 a.m.

he was the first boy
to teach me my body was
for giving to those that wanted
that i should feel anything
less than whole

and my god
did i feel as empty
as his mother at 4:25 a.m.

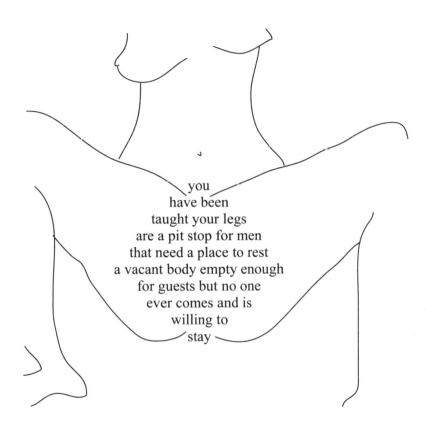

you
have been
taught your legs
are a pit stop for men
that need a place to rest
a vacant body empty enough
for guests but no one
ever comes and is
willing to
stay

it is your blood
in my veins
tell me how i'm
supposed to forget

the therapist places
the doll in front of you
it is the size of girls
your uncles like touching

point to where his hands were

you point to the spot
between its legs the one
he fingered out of you
like a confession

how're you feeling

you pull the lump
in your throat out
with your teeth
and say *fine*
numb really

- midweek sessions

he was supposed to be
the first male love of your life
you still search for him
everywhere

- *father*

you were so afraid
of my voice
i decided to be
afraid of it too

she was a rose
in the hands of those
who had no intention
of keeping her

every time you
tell your daughter
you yell at her
out of love
you teach her to confuse
anger with kindness
which seems like a good idea
till she grows up to
trust men who hurt her
cause they look so much
like you

- to fathers with daughters

i've had sex she said
but i don't know
what making love
feels like

if i knew what
safety looked like
i would have spent
less time falling into
arms that were not

sex takes the consent of two
if one person is lying there not doing anything
cause they are not ready
or not in the mood
or simply don't want to
yet the other is having sex
with their body it's not love
it is rape

the idea that we are
so capable of love
but still choose
to be toxic

there is no bigger illusion in the world
than the idea that a woman will
bring dishonor into a home
if she tries to keep her heart
and her body safe

you pinned
my legs to
the ground
with your feet
and demanded
i stand up

the rape will
tear you
in half

but it
will not
end you

you have sadness
living in places
sadness shouldn't live

a daughter should
not have to
beg her father
for a relationship

trying to convince myself
i am allowed
to take up space
is like writing with
my left hand
when i was born
to use my right

- *the idea of shrinking is hereditary*

you tell me to quiet down cause
my opinions make me less beautiful
but i was not made with a fire in my belly
so i could be put out
i was not made with a lightness on my tongue
so i could be easy to swallow
i was made heavy
half blade and half silk
difficult to forget and not easy
for the mind to follow

he guts her
with his fingers
like he's scraping
the inside of a
cantaloupe clean

your mother
is in the habit of
offering more love
than you can carry

your father is absent

you are a war
the border between two countries
the collateral damage
the paradox that joins the two
but also splits them apart

emptying out of my mother's belly
was my first act of disappearance
learning to shrink for a family
who likes their daughters invisible
was the second
the art of being empty
is simple
believe them when they say
you are nothing
repeat it to yourself
like a wish
i am nothing
i am nothing
i am nothing
so often
the only reason you know
you're still alive is from the
heaving of your chest

- *the art of being empty*

you look just like your mother

      i guess i do carry her tenderness well

you both have the same eyes

      cause we are both exhausted

and the hands

      we share the same wilting fingers

but that rage your mother doesn't wear that anger

      you're right
      this rage is the one thing
      i get from my father

(homage to warsan shire's *inheritance*)

when my mother opens her mouth
to have a conversation at dinner
my father shoves the word hush
between her lips and tells her to
never speak with her mouth full
this is how the women in my family
learned to live with their mouths closed

our knees
pried open
by cousins
and uncles
and men
our bodies touched
by all the wrong people
that even in a bed full of safety
we are afraid

father. you always call to say nothing in particular. you ask what i'm doing or where i am and when the silence stretches like a lifetime between us i scramble to find questions to keep the conversation going. what i long to say most is. i understand this world broke you. it has been so hard on your feet. i don't blame you for not knowing how to remain soft with me. sometimes i stay up thinking of all the places you are hurting which you'll never care to mention. i come from the same aching blood. from the same bone so desperate for attention i collapse in on myself. i am your daughter. i know the small talk is the only way you know how to tell me you love me. cause it is the only way i know how to tell you.

you plough into me with two fingers and i am mostly
shocked. it feels like rubber against an open wound.
i do not like it. you begin pushing faster and faster. but i
feel nothing. you search my face for a reaction so i begin
acting like the naked women in the videos you watch when
you think no one's looking. i imitate their moans. hollow
and hungry. you ask if it feels good and i say *yes*
so quickly it sounds rehearsed. but the acting.
you do not notice.

the thing about having
an alcoholic parent
is an alcoholic parent
does not exist

simply
an alcoholic
who could not stay sober
long enough to raise their kids

i can't tell if my mother is
terrified or in love with
my father it all
looks the same

i flinch when you touch me
i fear it is him

the
loving

when my mother was pregnant
with her second child i was four
i pointed at her swollen belly confused at how
my mother had gotten so big in such little time
my father scooped me in his tree trunk arms and
said the closest thing to god on this earth
is a woman's body it's where life comes from
and to have a grown man tell me something
so powerful at such a young age
changed me to see the entire universe
rested at my mother's feet

i struggle so deeply
to understand
how someone can
pour their entire soul
blood and energy
into someone
without wanting
anything in
return

- *i will have to wait till i'm a mother*

no
it won't
be love at
first sight when
we meet it'll be love
at first remembrance cause
i've seen you in my mother's eyes
when she tells me to marry the type
of man i'd want to raise my son to be like

every revolution
starts and ends
with his lips

what am i to you he asks
i put my hands in his lap
and whisper *you*
are every hope
i've ever had
in human form

my favorite thing about you is your smell
you smell like
earth
herbs
gardens
a little more
human than the rest of us

i know i
should crumble
for better reasons
but have you seen
that boy he brings
the sun to its
knees every
night

you are the faint line
between faith and
blindly waiting

- *letter to my future lover*

nothing is safer
than the sound of you
reading out loud to me

- the perfect date

he placed his hands
on my mind
before reaching
for my waist
my hips
or my lips
he didn't call me
beautiful first
he called me
exquisite

- *how he touches me*

i am learning
how to love him
by loving myself

he says
i am sorry i am not an easy person to want
i look at him surprised
who said i wanted easy
i don't crave easy
i crave goddamn difficult

the very thought of you
has my legs spread apart
like an easel with a canvas
begging for art

i am ready for you
i have always
been
ready for you

- *the first time*

i do not want to have you
to fill the empty parts of me
i want to be full on my own
i want to be so complete
i could light a whole city
and then
i want to have you
cause the two of us combined
could set it on fire

love will come
and when love comes
love will hold you
love will call your name
and you will melt
sometimes though
love will hurt you but
love will never mean to
love will play no games
cause love knows life
has been hard enough already

i'd be lying if i said
you make me speechless
the truth is you make my
tongue so weak it forgets
what language to speak in

he asks me what i do
i tell him i work for a small company
that makes packaging for—
he stops me midsentence
no not what you do to pay the bills
what drives you crazy
what keeps you up at night

i tell him *i write*
he asks me to show him something
i take the tips of my fingers
place them inside his forearm
and graze them down his wrist
goose bumps rise to the surface
i see his mouth clench
muscles tighten
his eyes pore into mine
as though i'm the reason
for making them blink
i break gaze just as
he inches toward me
i step back

so that's what you do
you command attention
my cheeks flush as
i smile shyly
confessing
i can't help it

you might not have been my first love
but you were the love that made
all the other loves
irrelevant

you've touched me
without even
touching me

how do you turn
a forest fire like me
so soft i turn into
running water

you look like you smell of
honey and no pain
let me have a taste of that

your name is
the strongest
positive and negative
connotation in any language
it either lights me up or
leaves me aching for days

you talk too much
he whispers into my ear
i can think of better ways to use that mouth

it's your voice
that undresses me

my name sounds so good
french kissing your tongue

you wrap your fingers
around my hair
and pull
this
is how you make
music out of me

- *foreplay*

on days
like this
i need you to
run your fingers
through my hair
and speak softly

- *you*

i want your hands
to hold
not my hands
your lips
to kiss
not my lips
but other places

i need someone
who knows struggle
as well as i do
someone
willing to hold my feet in their lap
on days it is too difficult to stand
the type of person who gives
exactly what i need
before i even know i need it
the type of lover who hears me
even when i do not speak
is the type of understanding
i demand

- *the type of lover i need*

you move my hand
between my legs
and whisper
make those pretty little fingers dance for me

- solo performance

we've been arguing more than we ought to. about things
neither of us remember or care about cause that's how
we avoid the bigger questions. instead of asking why we
don't say *i love you* to one another as often as we used to.
we fight about things like: who was supposed to get up
and turn the lights off first. or who was supposed to pop
the frozen pizza in the oven after work. taking hits at the
most vulnerable parts of one another. we're like fingers on
thorns honey. we know exactly where it hurts.

and everything is on the table tonight. like that one time
you whispered a name i'm pretty sure wasn't mine in your
sleep. or last week when you said you were working late.
so i called work but they said you'd already left a couple
hours ago. where were you for those couple hours.

i know. i know. your excuses make all the sense in the
world. and i get a little carried away for no good reason
and eventually begin crying. but what else do you expect
baby. i love you so much. i'm sorry i thought you were
lying.

that's when you hold your head with your hands in
frustration. half begging me to stop. half tired and sick of
it. the toxin in our mouths has burnt holes in our cheeks.
we look less alive than we used to. less color in our faces.
but don't kid yourself. no matter how bad it gets we both
know you still wanna nail me to the ground.

especially when i'm screaming so loud our fighting wakes
the neighbors. and they come running to the door to save
us. baby don't open it.

instead. lie me down. lay me open like a map. and with
your finger trace the places you still want to **** out of
me. kiss me like i am the center point of gravity and you
are falling into me like my soul is the focal point of yours.
and when your mouth is kissing not my mouth
but other places. my legs will split apart out of habit. and
that's when. i pull you in. welcome you. home.

when the entire street is looking out their windows
wondering what all the commotion is. and the fire trucks
come rolling in to save us but they can't distinguish
whether these flames began with our anger or our passion.
i will smile. throw my head back. arch my body like a
mountain you want to split in half. baby lick me.

like your mouth has the gift of reading and i'm your
favorite book. find your favorite page in the soft spot
between my legs and read it carefully. fluently. vividly.
don't you dare leave a single word untouched. and i swear
my ending will be so good. the last few words will come.
running to your mouth. and when you're done. take a
seat. cause it's my turn to make music with my knees
pressed to the ground.

sweet baby. this. is how we pull language out of one
another with the flick of our tongues. this is how we have
the conversation. this. is how we make up.

- *how we make up*

the
breaking

i always
get myself
into this mess
i always let him
tell me i am beautiful
and half believe it
i always jump thinking
he will catch me
at the fall
i am hopelessly
a lover and
a dreamer and
that will be the
death of me

when my mother says i deserve better
i snap to your defense out of habit
he still loves me i shout
she looks at me with defeated eyes
the way a parent looks at their child
when they know this is the type of pain
even they can't fix
and says
it means nothing to me if he loves you
if he can't do a single wretched thing about it

you were so distant
i forgot you were there at all

you said. if it is meant to be. fate will bring us back
together. for a second i wonder if you are really
that naive. if you really believe fate works like
that. as if it lives in the sky staring down at us. as
if it has five fingers and spends its time placing us
like pieces of chess. as if it is not the choices we
make. who taught you that. tell me. who
convinced you. you've been given a heart and
a mind that isn't yours to use. that your actions
do not define what will become of you. i want to
scream and shout *it's us you fool. we're the only*
ones that can bring us back together. but
instead i sit quietly. smiling softly through
quivering lips thinking. isn't it such a tragic thing.
when you can see it so clearly but the other person
doesn't.

don't mistake
salt for sugar
if he wants to
be with you
he will
it's that simple

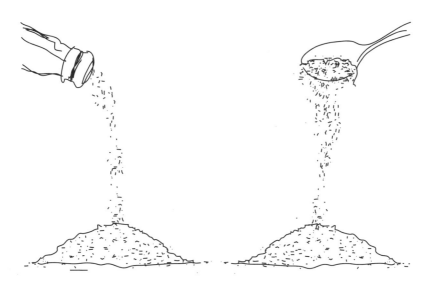

he only whispers *i love you*
as he slips his hands
down the waistband
of your pants

this is where you must
understand the difference
between want and need
you may want that boy
but you certainly
don't need him

you were temptingly beautiful
but stung when i got close

the woman who comes after me will be a bootleg
version of who i am. she will try and write poems
for you to erase the ones i've left memorized on
your lips but her lines could never punch you in
the stomach the way mine did. she will then try to
make love to your body. but she will never
lick, caress, or suck like me. she will be a sad
replacement of the woman you let slip. nothing she
does will excite you and this will break her. when
she is tired of falling apart for a man that doesn't
give back what he takes she will recognize me in
your eyelids staring at her with pity and it'll hit her.
how can she love a man who is busy loving
someone he can never get his hands on again.

the next time you
have your coffee black
you'll taste the bitter
state he left you in
it will make you weep
but you'll never
stop drinking
you'd rather have the
darkest parts of him
than have nothing

more than anything
i want to save you
from myself

you have spent enough nights
with his manhood curled inside your legs
to forget what loneliness feels like

you whisper
i love you
what you mean is
i don't want you to leave

that's the
thing about love
it marinates your lips
till the only word your
mouth remembers
is his name

it must hurt to know
i am your most
beautiful
regret

i didn't leave because
i stopped loving you
i left because the longer
i stayed the less
i loved myself

you mustn't have to
make them want you
they must want you themselves

did you think i was a city
big enough for a weekend getaway
i am the town surrounding it
the one you've never heard of
but always pass through
there are no neon lights here
no skyscrapers or statues
but there is thunder
for i make bridges tremble
i am not street meat i am homemade jam
thick enough to cut the sweetest
thing your lips will touch
i am not police sirens
i am the crackle of a fireplace
i'd burn you and you still
couldn't take your eyes off me
cause i'd look so beautiful doing it
you'd blush
i am not a hotel room i am home
i am not the whiskey you want
i am the water you need
don't come here with expectations
and try to make a vacation out of me

the one who arrives after you
will remind me love is
supposed to be soft

he will taste
like the poetry
i wish i could write

if
he can't help but
degrade other women
when they're not looking
if toxicity is central
to his language
he could hold you
in his lap and be soft
honey
that man could feed you sugar and
douse you in rose water
but that still could not
make him sweet

- *if you want to know the type of man he is*

i am a museum full of art
but you had your eyes shut

you must have known
you were wrong
when your fingers
were dipped inside me
searching for honey that
would not come for you

the thing
worth holding on to
would not have let go

when you are broken
and he has left you
do not question
whether you were
enough
the problem was
you were so enough
he was not able to carry it

love made the danger
in you look like safety

even when you undress her
you are searching for me
i am sorry i
taste so good
when the two of you
make love it is
still my name
that rolls off your
tongue accidently

you treat them like they
have a heart like yours
but not everyone can be as
soft and as tender

you don't see the
person they are
you see the person
they have the potential to be

you give and give till
they pull everything out of you
and leave you empty

i had to leave
i was tired of
allowing you to
make me feel
anything less
than whole

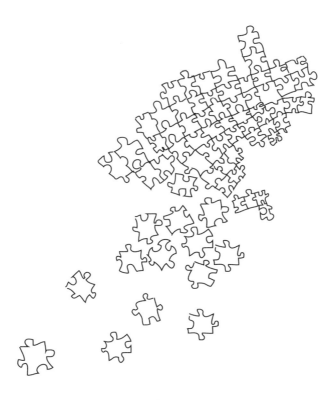

you were the most beautiful thing i'd ever felt till now. and i was convinced you'd remain the most beautiful thing i'd ever feel. do you know how limiting that is. to think at such a ripe young age i'd experienced the most exhilarating person i'd ever meet. how i'd spend the rest of my life just settling. to think i'd tasted the rawest form of honey and everything else would be refined and synthetic. that nothing beyond this point would add up. that all the years beyond me could not combine themselves to be sweeter than you.

- *falsehood*

i don't know what living a balanced life feels like
when i am sad
i don't cry i pour
when i am happy
i don't smile i glow
when i am angry
i don't yell i burn

the good thing about feeling in extremes is
when i love i give them wings
but perhaps that isn't
such a good thing cause
they always tend to leave
and you should see me
when my heart is broken
i don't grieve
i shatter

i came all this way
to give you all these things
but you aren't even looking

the abused
and the
abuser

- *i have been both*

i am undoing you
from my skin

it wasn't you i was kissing
— don't be mistaken

it was him on my mind
your lips were just convenient

it always comes back to you
boils
circles
itches
its way back to you

i was music
but you had your ears cut off

my tongue is sour
from the hunger of
missing you

i will not have you
build me into your life
when
what i want is to
build a life with you

- the difference

rivers fall from my mouth
tears my eyes can't carry

you are snakeskin
and i keep shedding you somehow
my mind is forgetting
every exquisite detail
of your face
the letting go has
become the forgetting
which is the most
pleasant and saddest thing
to have happened

you were not wrong for leaving
you were wrong for coming back
and thinking
you could have me
when it was convenient
and leave when it was not

how can i write
if he took my hands
with him

neither of us is happy
but neither of us wants to leave
so we keep breaking one another
and calling it love

we began
with honesty
let us end
in it too

- *us*

your voice
alone
drives me
to tears

i don't know why
i split myself open
for others knowing
sewing myself up
hurts this much
afterward

people go
but how
they left
always stays

love is not cruel
we are cruel
love is not a game
we have made a game
out of love

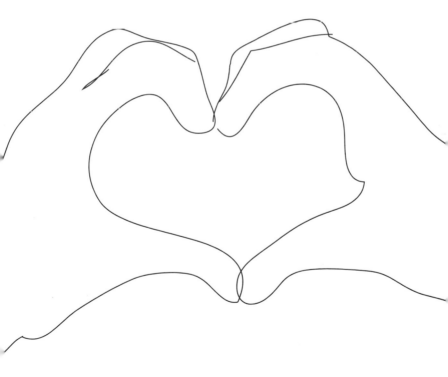

how can our love die
if it's written
in these pages

even after the hurt
the loss
the pain
the breaking
your body is still
the only one
i want to be
undressed under

the night after you left
i woke up so broken
the only place to put the pieces
were the bags under my eyes

stay
i whispered
as you
shut the door behind you

i am confident i am over you. so much that some
mornings i wake up with a smile on my face and
my hands pressed together thanking the universe
for pulling you out of me. thank god i cry. thank
god you left. i would not be the empire i am today
if you had stayed.

but then.

there are some nights i imagine what i might do if
you showed up. how if you walked into the room
this very second every awful thing you've ever
done would be tossed out the closest window and
all the love would rise up again. it would pour
through my eyes as if it never really left in the first
place. as if it's been practicing how to stay silent
so long only so it could be this loud on your arrival.
can someone explain that. how even when the love
leaves. it doesn't leave. how even when i am so
past you. i am so helplessly brought back to you.

he isn't coming back
whispered my head
he has to
sobbed my heart

- *wilting*

i don't want to be friends
i want all of you

- *more*

i am losing parts of you like i lose eyelashes
unknowingly and everywhere

you cannot leave
and have me too
i cannot exist in
two places at once

- *when you ask if we can still be friends*

i am water

soft enough
to offer life
tough enough
to drown it away

what i miss most is how you loved me. but what i didn't
know was how you loved me had so much to do with
the person i was. it was a reflection of everything i gave
to you. coming back to me. how did i not see that. how.
did i sit here soaking in the idea that no one else would
love me that way. when it was i that taught you. when it
was i that showed you how to fill. the way i needed to be
filled. how cruel i was to myself. giving you credit for my
warmth simply because you had felt it. thinking it was
you who gave me strength. wit. beauty. simply because
you recognized it. as if i was already not these things
before i met you. as if i did not remain all these once you
left.

you leave
but you don't stay gone
why do you do that
why do you
abandon the thing you want to keep
why do you linger
in a place you do not want to stay
why do you think it's okay to do both
go and return all at once

i will tell you about selfish people. even when they know
they will hurt you they walk into your life to taste you
because you are the type of being they don't want to miss
out on. you are too much shine to not be felt. so when they
have gotten a good look at everything you have to offer.
when they have taken your skin your hair your secrets with
them. when they realize how real this is. how much of a
storm you are and it hits them.

that is when the cowardice sets in. that is when the person
you thought they were is replaced by the sad reality of
what they are. that is when they lose every fighting bone in
their body and leave after saying *you will find better than
me.*

you will stand there naked with half of them still hidden
somewhere inside you and sob. asking them why they did
it. why they forced you to love them when they had no
intention of loving you back and they'll say something
along the lines of *i just had to try. i had to give it a chance.
it was you after all.*

but that isn't romantic. it isn't sweet. the idea that they
were so engulfed by your existence they had to risk
breaking it for the sake of knowing they weren't the one
missing out. your existence meant that little next to their
curiosity of you.

that is the thing about selfish people. they
gamble entire beings. entire souls to please their
own. one second they are holding you like the
world in their lap and the next they have
belittled you to a mere picture. a moment.
something of the past. one second. they swallow
you up and whisper they want to spend the rest
of their life with you. but the moment they sense
fear. they are already halfway out the door.
without having the nerve to let you go with
grace. as if the human heart means that little to
them.

and after all this. after all of the taking. the
nerve. isn't it sad and funny how people have
more guts these days to undress you with their
fingers than they do to pick up the phone and
call. apologize. for the loss. and this is how you
lose her.

- *selfish*

to do list (after the breakup):

1. take refuge in your bed.
2. cry. till the tears stop (this will take a few days).
3. don't listen to slow songs.
4. delete their number from your phone even though it is memorized on your fingertips.
5. don't look at old photos.
6. find the closest ice cream shop and treat yourself to two scoops of mint chocolate chip. the mint will calm your heart. you deserve the chocolate.
7. buy new bed sheets.
8. collect all the gifts, t-shirts, and everything with their smell on it and drop it off at a donation center.
9. plan a trip.
10. perfect the art of smiling and nodding when someone brings their name up in conversation.
11. start a new project.
12. whatever you do. do not call.
13. do not beg for what does not want to stay.
14. stop crying at some point.
15. allow yourself to feel foolish for believing you could've built the rest of your life in someone else's stomach.
16. breathe.

the way they
leave
tells you
everything

the
healing

perhaps
i don't deserve
nice things
cause i am paying
for sins i don't
remember

the thing about writing is
i can't tell if it's healing
or destroying me

do not bother holding on to
that thing that does not want you

- you cannot make it stay

you must enter a relationship
with yourself
before anyone else

accept that you deserve more
than painful love
life is moving
the healthicst thing
for your heart is
to move with it

it is a part of the
human experience to feel pain
do not be afraid
open yourself to it

- *evolving*

loneliness is a sign you are in desperate need of yourself

you are in the habit
of co-depending
on people to
make up for what
you think you lack

who tricked you
into believing
another person
was meant to complete you
when the most they can do is complement

do not look for healing
at the feet of those
who broke you

if you were born with
the weakness to fall
you were born with
the strength to rise

perhaps the saddest of all
are those who live waiting
for someone they're not
sure exists

- 7 billion people

stay strong through your pain
grow flowers from it
you have helped me
grow flowers out of mine so
bloom beautifully
dangerously
loudly
bloom softly
however you need
just bloom

- *to the reader*

i thank the universe
for taking
everything it has taken
and giving to me
everything it is giving

- *balance*

it takes grace
to remain kind
in cruel situations

fall
in love
with your solitude

there is a difference between
someone telling you
they love you and
them actually
loving you

sometimes
the apology
never comes
when it is wanted

and when it comes
it is neither wanted
nor needed

- *you are too late*

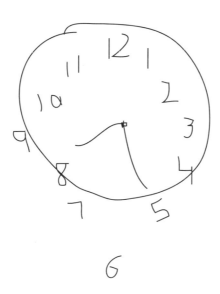

you tell me
i am not like most girls
and learn to kiss me with your eyes closed
something about the phrase—something about
how i have to be unlike the women
i call sisters in order to be wanted
makes me want to spit your tongue out
like i am supposed to be proud you picked me
as if i should be relieved you think
i am better than them

the next time he
points out the
hair on your legs is
growing back remind
that boy your body
is not his home
he is a guest
warn him to
never outstep
his welcome
again

to be
soft
is
to be
powerful

you deserve to be
completely found
in your surroundings
not lost within them

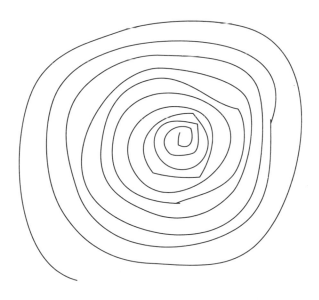

i know it's hard
believe me
i know it feels like
tomorrow will never come
and today will be the most
difficult day to get through
but i swear you will get through
the hurt will pass
as it always does
if you give it time and
let it so let it
go
slowly
like a broken promise
let it go

i like the way the stretch marks
on my thighs look human and
that we're so soft yet
rough and jungle wild
when we need to be
i love that about us
how capable we are of feeling
how unafraid we are of breaking
and tend to our wounds with grace
just being a woman
calling myself
a woman
makes me utterly whole
and complete

my issue with what they consider beautiful
is their concept of beauty
centers around excluding people
i find hair beautiful
when a woman wears it
like a garden on her skin
that is the definition of beauty
big hooked noses
pointing upward to the sky
like they're rising
to the occasion
skin the color of earth
my ancestors planted crops on
to feed a lineage of women with
thighs thick as tree trunks
eyes like almonds
deeply hooded with conviction
the rivers of punjab
flow through my bloodstream so
don't tell me my women
aren't as beautiful
as the ones in
your country

our backs
tell stories
no books have
the spine to
carry

- women of color

accept yourself
as you were designed

your body
is a museum
of natural disasters
can you grasp how
stunning that is

losing you
was the becoming
of myself

other women's bodies
are not our battlegrounds

removing all the hair
off your body is okay
if that's what you want to do
just as much as keeping all the hair
on your body is okay
if that's what you want to do

- *you belong only to yourself*

apparently it is ungraceful of me
to mention my period in public
cause the actual biology
of my body is too real

it is okay to sell what's
between a woman's legs
more than it is okay to
mention its inner workings

the recreational use of
this body is seen as
beautiful while
its nature is
seen as ugly

you were a dragon long before
he came around and said
you could fly

you will remain a dragon
long after he's left

i want to apologize to all the women
i have called pretty
before i've called them intelligent or brave
i am sorry i made it sound as though
something as simple as what you're born with
is the most you have to be proud of when your
spirit has crushed mountains
from now on i will say things like
you are resilient or *you are extraordinary*
not because i don't think you're pretty
but because you are so much more than that

i have
what i have
and i am happy

i've lost
what i've lost
and i am
still
happy

- *outlook*

you look at me and cry
everything hurts

i hold you and whisper
but everything can heal

if the hurt comes
so will the happiness

- *be patient*

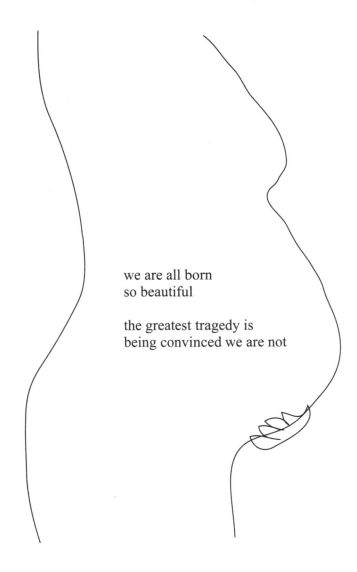

we are all born
so beautiful

the greatest tragedy is
being convinced we are not

the name kaur
makes me a free woman
it removes the shackles that
try to bind me
uplifts me
to remind me i am equal to
any man even though the state
of this world screams to me i am not
that i am my own woman and
i belong wholly to myself
and the universe
it humbles me
calls out and says i have a
universal duty to share with
humanity to nurture
and serve the sisterhood
to raise those that need raising
the name kaur runs in my blood
it was in me before the word itself existed
it is my identity and my liberation

- *kaur*
  a woman of sikhi

the world
gives you
so much pain
and here you are
making gold out of it

- there is nothing purer than that

how you love yourself is
how you teach others
to love you

my heart aches for sisters more than anything
it aches for women helping women
like flowers ache for spring

the goddess between your legs
makes mouths water

you
are your own
soul mate

some people
are so bitter

to them
you must be kindest

we all move forward when
we recognize how resilient
and striking the women
around us are

for you to see beauty here
does not mean
there is beauty in me
it means there is beauty rooted
so deep within you
you can't help but
see it everywhere

hair
if it was not supposed to be there
would not be growing
on our bodies in the first place

- we are at war with what comes most naturally to us

most importantly love
like it's the only thing you know how
at the end of the day all this
means nothing
this page
where you're sitting
your degree
your job
the money
nothing even matters
except love and human connection
who you loved
and how deeply you loved them
how you touched the people around you
and how much you gave them

i want to remain so
rooted to the ground
these tears
these hands
these feet
sink in

- grounded

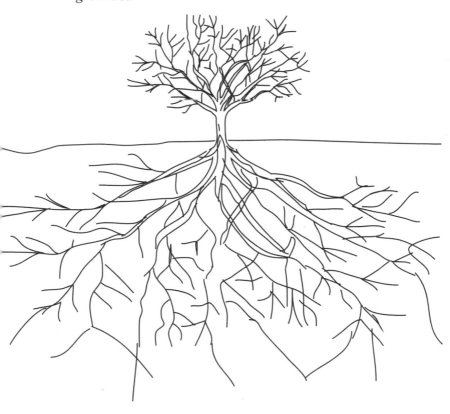

you have to stop
searching for why at some point
you have to leave it alone

if you are not enough for yourself
you will never be enough
for someone else

you must
want to spend
the rest of your life
with yourself
first

of course i want to be successful
but i don't crave success for me
i need to be successful to gain
enough milk and honey
to help those around
me succeed

my heartbeat quickens at
the thought of birthing poems
which is why i will never stop
opening myself up to conceive them
the lovemaking
to the words
is so erotic
i am either in love
or in lust with
the writing
or both

what terrifies me most is how we
foam at the mouth with envy
when others succeed
but sigh in relief
when they are failing

our struggle to
celebrate each other is
what's proven most difficult
in being human

your art
is not about how many people
like your work
your art
is about
if your heart likes your work
if your soul likes your work
it's about how honest
you are with yourself
and you
must never
trade honesty
for relatability

- to all you young poets

give to those
who have nothing
to give to you

- *seva (selfless service)*

you split me open
in the most honest
way there is
to split a soul open
and forced me to write
at a time i was sure i
could not write again

- *thank you*

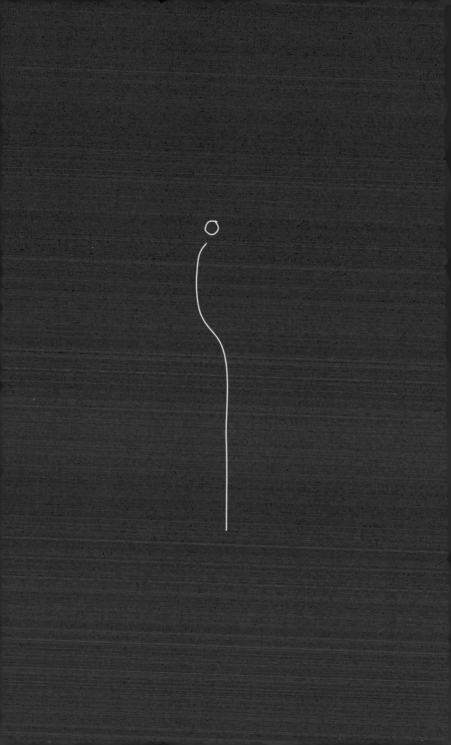

you have made it to the end. with my heart in your hands. thank you. for arriving here safely. for being tender with the most delicate part of me. sit down. breathe. you must be tired. let me kiss your hands. your eyes. they must be wanting of something sweet. i am sending you all my sugar. i would be nowhere and nothing if it were not for you. you've helped me become the woman i wanted to be. but was too afraid to be. do you have any idea how much of a miracle you are. how lovely it's been. and how lovely it will always be. i am kneeling before you. saying thank you. i am sending my love to your eyes. may they always see goodness in people. and may you always practice kindness. may we see each other as one. may we be nothing short of in love with everything the universe has to offer. and may we always stay grounded. rooted. our feet planted firmly onto the earth.

- a love letter from me to you

when she was five her mother handed her a
paintbrush and said - draw your heart out.
rupi kaur views her life as an exploration of that
artistic journey. through her poetry and illustra-
tions she engages with love loss trauma healing
and femininity. for rupi writing has always been
a collective experience. at the age of seventeen
she began sharing her work. the stage was her
first love and spoken word is where she found
her voice. rupi pursued her love for language by
studying rhetoric at the university of waterloo.
she began working on her first collection *milk
and honey* which eventually became a *new york
times* bestseller. rupi's passion is expression.
for her that expression is taking many forms.
her photography and art direction are brought to
various spaces around the world and her poetry
and prose are breaking international boundaries.

- *about the writer*

milk and honey is a
collection of poetry about
love
loss
trauma
abuse
healing
and femininity
it is split into four chapters
each chapter serves a different purpose
deals with a different pain
heals a different heartache
milk and honey takes readers through
a journey of the most bitter moments in life
and finds sweetness in them
because there is sweetness everywhere
if you are just willing to look

- *about the book*